Vidia and the Fairy Crown

This edition published by Parragon in 2011

Parragon
Queen Street House
4 Queen Street
Bath, BA1 1HE, UK

ISBN 978-1-4454-5028-5

Printed in China.

Vidia and the Fairy Crown

WRITTEN BY

Laura Driscoll

ILLUSTRATED BY

Judith Holmes Clarke

&

The Disney Storybook Artists

Bath · New York · Singapore · Hong Kong · Cologne · Delhi
Melbourne · Amsterdam · Johannesburg · Auckland · Shenzhen

Come one, come every Never fairy
and every sparrow man to
Her Royal Majesty Queen Clarion's
Arrival Day Bash!

~ where ~
The Home Tree Dining Hall

~ when ~
The evening of the next full
moon, just after sunset

To make it the merriest,
wear your fairy best!

Every fairy and sparrow man in Pixie Hollow had received the same invitation. It was handwritten on linen in blackberry juice.

It was going to be the biggest celebration Pixie Hollow had seen in a long time. The Never fairies were going to celebrate the Arrival Day of their beloved queen, Clarion, whose nickname was Ree.

In the kitchen, on the ground floor of the Home Tree, the cooking-and-baking-talent fairies were whipping up a seven-course royal Arrival Day dinner. Dulcie, a baking-talent fairy, was churning out batch after batch of her speciality – the most delicious poppy puff rolls in all of Never Land. And, of course, there was strawberry-seed cake, too.

The decoration-talent fairies and the celebration-setup fairies zipped about the dining hall.

They draped
the tables with
gold tablecloths
and delicate lacy
spiderwebs. They
hung colourful
balloons in the
arched doorway.
They sprinkled flower-
petal confetti on every table
and across the floor.

Meanwhile, the sewing-talent
fairies put the finishing touches on
the queen's dress. They decorated it

8

with pale pink rose petals, soft green leaves and freshwater pearls.

Even Tinker Bell, a member of the tinker-talent, was helping out. The cooking-talent fairies needed every pot and pan they could get their hands on. So Tinker Bell fixed all the broken pots in her workshop. Then she returned them all to the kitchen.

On her last trip down, Tink met up with her friend Rani, a water-talent fairy.

"Rani!" Tink called. "Do you have time for a break?"

"Yes," Rani replied. "I do have time."

They stepped out into the late-morning sunshine.

Tink took a deep breath of fresh air. "It's going to be a beautiful –"

"– evening," said Rani, finishing the thought. "The perfect night for a party."

Just then, there was a rustling in the brush overhead. Both Tink and Rani jumped.

"Is it a hawk?" Rani cried in alarm.

"That's no hawk," Tink said with a laugh. "It's Vidia."

A dark-haired fairy zipped down from above. She landed next to Tink and Rani.

"Hello, darlings," Vidia said. She flashed them a sly smile. "Why aren't you two inside getting ready for the big party – just like all the other good fairies?" Vidia asked them.

"We were," Tinker Bell replied shortly. "We're –"

"– taking a break," said Rani.

"What's *your* excuse?" Tinker Bell asked Vidia.

Tinker Bell knew all too well that Vidia wouldn't be helping out that day. Vidia's relationship with Queen Ree was... complicated. In fact, Vidia's relationship with *everyone* in Pixie Hollow was complicated. Vidia lived far from the other fairies in a sour-plum tree and kept to herself.

"Are you even *coming* to the party tonight?" Tinker Bell asked Vidia.

Vidia smiled. "To the queen's party?" She laughed mockingly. "Of course not, dear." Vidia paused and seemed to consider a new thought. "Oh, unless you need someone to fly in and snatch that gaudy crown off high and mighty Queen Ree's head," she said. "Now, *that* sounds like fun. In fact, that's quite a tempting idea – party or no party." Vidia shrugged. "Ah, well. You two dears have fun tonight!"

With that, Vidia took to the air. In a flash, she was gone.

That evening the queen's four helper fairies – Cinda, Rhia, Lisel

and Grace – were laying out the
clothes, shoes and jewellery that Ree
would wear to the party.

Lisel gently took the queen's fancy
new gown from the closet and put it
on the queen's bed. Grace picked out
a pair of heels for the queen to wear.
Rhia chose a pretty shell charm on a
silver chain.

Cinda entered the queen's sitting room and crossed to the crown cabinet on a side table. It was traditional for the queen to wear her crown to any celebration. The crown was the most special fairy treasure in all of Pixie Hollow. It had been passed down from fairy queen to fairy queen. It could not be replaced.

So when she opened the cabinet, Cinda froze.

The crown wasn't there.

When Queen Ree heard the news of the missing crown, she called an emergency meeting. She watched as fairies flew into the clearing.

"What do you think is wrong?" whispered one fairy.

"It must be an emergency," whispered another, "or it wouldn't be called an 'emergency meeting'."

The fairies gathered in a wide circle around Ree.

Soon the courtyard was bright with the glows of hundreds of Never fairies and sparrow men. Even Vidia was there. She lurked in the shadows of a mulberry bush. At last, Ree cleared her throat. All the fairies and sparrow men fell silent.

"Fairies! Sparrow men!" the queen called out. "I have called this meeting to let you all know that there will be no celebration tonight."

A murmur arose from the crowd. The fairies exchanged puzzled glances.

"I need your help in finding my crown, which has gone missing today," the queen went on. At that, the crowd's murmur became a cry of alarm.

"Do you mean that someone has *stolen* the crown?" Tink called out from her perch on a tree root.

"Now, now," said the queen, trying to calm the crowd. "Let's not jump to any conclusions."

"Where was it last seen?" asked Terence, a fairy-dust-talent sparrow man.

"Who was the last fairy to see it?" added Tink.

"How long has it been gone?" asked Iridessa, a light-talent fairy.

Queen Ree held up her hands to quiet the crowd. "Those are all good questions," she said. "We don't have answers for all of them yet. But maybe

I should ask my helper fairy Cinda to come forward. She is the one who noticed that the crown was missing."

Cinda flew to the centre of the courtyard and stood at the queen's side.

"Well, there's not much to tell," she said quietly. "I thought maybe another fairy had already taken the crown out and laid it on the queen's dressing table. But when I asked the others if they knew where the crown was, no one did!" Cinda looked up at the queen.

Then, as Cinda retook her place in the circle of fairies, the queen looked up at the crowd. "Now I have something to ask all of you," she said. "Has anyone seen or heard anything recently that might have something to do with the missing crown?"

"Well," said Tink, "Vidia said she was planning to fly into Queen Ree's party –"

"– and snatch the crown off her head," Rani finished.

All eyes turned toward Vidia, who crossed her arms. She scowled across the fairy circle at Rani and Tink.

"Well?" said Queen Ree, turning to look at Vidia. "Is that true?"

"I said I wasn't coming to the party," Vidia replied. "I think my exact words were 'unless, of course, you need

someone to fly in and snatch that gaudy crown off high-and-mighty Queen Ree's head.'"

The crowd gasped. To say such

a thing – and right in front of the queen herself! Then again, Vidia had never been one to mince words.

"That's not all," Tinker Bell said. "Then you said that the idea of snatching the crown sounded like fun – that it was something to consider –"

"– party or no party," said Rani, finishing Tink's sentence.

Vidia forced a laugh. "Oh, this is ridiculous," she said. "Yes, I said those things. But, really, what would I want with your crown? What would I do with it? It's not like I could steal it and then fly around wearing it, could I?"

Queen Ree looked troubled. "No, Vidia," she replied. "That doesn't make sense. I have no idea what you would do with the crown. And I don't want to believe that you had anything to do with its disappearance. But these are serious charges."

The queen looked around at all the fairies and sparrow men. "Does anyone else have any other information to share?" she asked.

No one spoke.

"Well, then," the queen said. She turned back to Vidia. "I have no choice. The crown is special to all of us. It doesn't belong to me. It belongs to Pixie Hollow. If we should find that anyone here has taken it..." She took a deep breath before continuing. "I think we would have to call it an act of treason," she said sadly. "And the only fitting punishment for such a crime is lifetime banishment from Pixie Hollow."

Vidia's mouth dropped open in shock. "This is unbelievable!" she cried. "Don't I even get a chance to defend myself? Can't I prove that I didn't do it?"

"Of course you can," Queen Ree replied. "But not tonight. It's late. We're all tired." The queen took to the air. She hovered above the crowd. "Let's all gather again the day after tomorrow," she added. "We'll hold Vidia's hearing then, mid-morning. Everyone who wishes to come may do so. And, Vidia, you will have the chance to speak to the charges against you." Queen Ree nodded solemnly and brought the meeting to a close.

3

Vidia was still in shock. She sat on the ground in the shadow of a mulberry bush and stared blankly ahead of her. She made no move to go until it seemed she was all alone. Then, with a heavy sigh, she stood up and turned around – and saw Prilla sitting on a toadstool on the far side of the courtyard.

Prilla was fairly new to Pixie

Hollow. She hadn't known Vidia as long as some others had. But she had been on a grand adventure with her and got to know her better than most fairies did.

Maybe that was part of the reason

Prilla stayed behind when the emergency meeting ended. Unlike some of the other fairies, Prilla didn't believe that Vidia was all bad.

"Vidia, are you okay?" Prilla asked. She flew over and landed at the fast-flying fairy's side.

Vidia waved Prilla away. "Oh, save your pity, sweetheart," she replied. She forced a smile, but it quickly faded. "Do you think I'm worried? Well, think again. There's a reason I live on my own in the sour-plum tree. It's because I find all of you very irritating. What do I care if I'm banished from Pixie Hollow? I can't stand the place."

Prilla didn't believe her. She could see the fear in Vidia's eyes. She knew that Vidia found Pixie Hollow annoying. But even Vidia wouldn't want to be forced to leave her home.

"I'll help you, Vidia," Prilla offered. "Tomorrow, we'll start an investigation. It's like a mystery that needs to be solved, don't you see?" Prilla jumped into the air and turned a somersault. "We'll be detectives!"

Vidia wrinkled her brow and looked sideways at Prilla. "And how do you know I *didn't* take the crown?"

Prilla landed and shrugged. "I just don't think you did."

"And *why* do you want to help me, dearest?" Vidia asked.

Prilla thought it over for a moment. When she'd first arrived in Pixie Hollow, she'd had trouble figuring out what her talent was. In the end, Prilla had learned that she was the only fairy with her particular talent. She was the first mainland-visiting clapping-talent fairy ever. Over time, Prilla had settled into life in Pixie Hollow. She had made lots of new friends. She had found her place. But she still remembered those early days.

Prilla looked Vidia in the eye. "I want to help you," she said, "because I remember what it's like to feel alone."

Vidia returned Prilla's gaze and then looked away. She cleared her throat. She looked up at the stars. "Okay," she said at last.

It was barely a whisper. But Prilla heard it, and she understood.

Vidia and Prilla met after breakfast the next morning.

"Come on," Vidia barked. "We'll start with the queen's helpers."

Prilla struggled to keep up as she followed Vidia to the queen's quarters.

Vidia rushed into the queen's sitting room without waiting to be invited in. All the helper fairies were there.

"What a brave little fairy you were last night, Cinda darling – coming forward to tell your tale in front of that big, scary crowd." Vidia flashed Cinda a sickly sweet smile. "But we have just a few more questions to ask you and your fellow helper fairies. Don't we, Prilla?"

Prilla flew forwards and tried to smooth things over. She could see that the queen's helpers were not happy to have Vidia in the queen's quarters. "We'd just like to ask you some questions about yesterday," Prilla said hopefully, "so we can prepare Vidia's defence for tomorrow."

"'*We*'?" said Grace, her eyes wide with surprise. "Prilla, are you actually *helping* her?"

Prilla shrugged and her glow flared. "Yes," she replied. "There's no proof that Vidia took the crown."

"No proof *yet,*" Lisel muttered under her breath. She set the sheets and pillowcases down, and the helpers began folding them.

"Listen, dearies," Vidia said. She flew across the room to hover over the helpers as they folded. "All I want to know is when each of you last saw the crown."

Cinda shook the wrinkles out of a pillowcase. "I saw the crown yesterday

morning," she said. "Rhia took it out
of the cabinet to make sure it was
ready for the party. Right, Rhia?"

"Right," Rhia replied. "I took the
crown out and started to clean it.
Then I noticed that there was a small
dent in the metal, so I took the crown

up to the crown-repair workshop to have it fixed."

Vidia flew excitedly to Rhia's side. "And when was this?" Vidia asked.

"Yesterday morning," Rhia said. She described how she had put the crown in its black velvet carrying pouch, taken it up to the crown-repair workshop and left it with Aidan, the crown-repair sparrow man. "I told him to bring it back to the queen's chambers when he was done."

"I see," Vidia replied. "And he did?"

Rhia nodded confidently. "Yes," she said. Then her brow wrinkled. "I mean, I think so." Her glow flared. "Well, actually, I don't know for *sure*."

The three other helper fairies stopped folding. They stared at Rhia. "Rhia," said Lisel in shock, "what do you mean you don't know for *sure?*"

"Well... I... I mean," Rhia stammered, "I told him he could leave it with any one of us, whoever was here." Rhia's eyes searched her friends' faces. "Didn't any of you see him bring it back yesterday?" she asked hopefully.

Lisel shook her head.

"Not me," said Grace.

"Me neither," said Cinda.

Rhia covered her mouth with her hand. It muffled the sound when she cried, "Oh, no!"

Prilla shot Vidia an "aha!" look.

Vidia zipped towards the door. "Come on, Prilla," she called behind her. "We have a crown-repair sparrow man to visit."

5

By the time Prilla caught up with Vidia, the fast-flyer was already questioning Aidan in the crown-repair workshop.

"What do you mean you didn't see the crown yesterday?" Vidia was shouting. "Rhia said she brought it to you to be fixed!"

"I did!" exclaimed a voice behind Prilla. She turned to find Rhia

standing in the doorway of
the workshop.

Aidan nervously scratched his
head. Moments before, he'd had his
quiet workshop all to himself – as he
did most days. Aidan's talent was a
specialised one. There weren't many
crowns in Pixie Hollow in need of
repair. In fact, there weren't many
crowns in Pixie Hollow at all!
So most of Aidan's time was spent
on his own, perfecting his crown-
repair skills.

"Please," said Aidan. "I – I'm
telling you the truth. I saw *Rhia*
yesterday, but I d-didn't see the
queen's crown."

Rhia flew across the workshop and landed at Aidan's side. "Don't you remember? I had asked you to bring it back to the queen's chambers when you were done," she said. "So why didn't you?"

Aidan's big green eyes had grown wider as Rhia told her story. "Is *that* why you came into my workshop yesterday?" he asked her. "Rhia, when you came in yesterday, I had just finished doing some work with my gemstone drill. It works well, but it makes a terrible racket. Here, I'll show you."

Aidan turned the drill's crank. A loud, high-pitched squeal filled the

workshop. Vidia, Prilla and Rhia covered their ears with their hands.

"Stop, stop, stop!" Vidia shouted over the noise. Aidan stopped drilling.

Prilla uncovered her ears. "Gosh, Aidan," she said. "How do you stand it?"

Aidan reached into the pockets of his baggy work trousers. "I use these," he replied, pulling his hands out of his pockets. He opened them to reveal several wads of dandelion fluff. Then he stuffed a wad in each ear to show how it worked.

"Let's cut to the chase," Vidia snapped impatiently. "What does all this have to do with the missing crown?"

"WHAT?" said Aidan loudly.

Vidia sighed and yanked the fluff out of his ears. "WHY DO I CARE ABOUT YOUR EARPLUGS?" she shouted.

Aidan shrank from Vidia. He turned towards Rhia instead. "Well, when you came in yesterday, I had my back to you. Didn't I?"

Rhia nodded.

"I still had the dandelion fluff in my ears," said Aidan, "because I was working with the drill." He shrugged. "So whatever you said, I didn't hear. When I turned and saw you standing in the doorway, I waved. Remember? But then you turned and left! So I figured you had just dropped by to say hello."

Rhia held her head in her hands. "And *I* thought you were waving to show that you had heard everything I'd said." She groaned. Then an idea came to her. "But whether you heard me or not, I *did* leave the crown here."

"Well, then," said Prilla hopefully, "it must be around here somewhere." She peeked under the table while Rhia checked inside some nearby cupboards.

But there was no crown or velvet pouch to be found.

Prilla sighed. "Aidan," she said, "did anyone else come into your workshop yesterday? Anyone besides Rhia?"

Aidan thought it over, then nodded. "Yes. Twire came by," he replied.

"Twire?" said Rhia. "The scrap-metal-recovery fairy?"

Aidan nodded. "She picked up yesterday's scrap metal. She melts it down and recycles it."

Prilla gasped.

Rhia groaned.

Vidia pursed her lips and shook her head.

"What?" said Aidan.

Vidia flashed Aidan her sickly sweet smile. "Don't you see, pet?" she said. "If the crown was on that table next to the scrap metal when Twire came to pick it up..."

"She might have taken the crown

away with the scrap metal..." Rhia
continued the thought.

Prilla gulped. "And melted
it down!"

The fastest fast-flying-talent fairy in Pixie Hollow rocketed out of Aidan's workshop and zipped towards Twire's.

Vidia barged through Twire's door without knocking and flew straight into a set of metal wind chimes that hung from the ceiling.

Prrriiinnnnnggggggg! The wind chimes rang forcefully as Vidia

plowed through them.

Across the workshop, a startled
Twire straightened up and took a
break from her task – dropping bits
of scrap aluminum and copper into a
large vat of molten metal.

"Stop!" Vidia called out. "Stop
what you're doing!"

"What's the matter?" Twire replied.

Just then Prilla arrived, slightly out of breath.

"The queen's crown!" Vidia snapped at Twire as she searched the workshop, tossing bits of metal here and there. "Have you seen it?"

Twire shook her head and removed her goggles. "No, Vidia. I haven't," she replied calmly.

Vidia gave up her search and sighed. She impatiently repeated what Aidan had said; that Twire had picked up his scrap metal the day before.

Twire nodded. "That's right," she said. "I brought it back here, sorted it and began to melt some pieces down."

Prilla watched as Vidia leaned over Twire menacingly. "And you're sure you didn't find anything unusual mixed in with the scrap metal?" she asked. "Think carefully, love. The crown might have been in a black velvet pouch."

At this, Twire started. "Velvet?" she said, her face brightening. "Yes! Yes, I did find some velvet in the pile."

"Tell me what you did with it!" Vidia snapped.

Twire sighed and flew towards a tiny door in the wall at the far side of the workshop. Vidia and Prilla followed.

"Well, I didn't know there was anything in it," Twire explained as she flew. "I was sure I could use the velvet for something. But it had a few rust stains on it. You know, from being around the metal. So I tossed it down the laundry chute."

Vidia took off so suddenly,
Prilla had to fly her fastest to catch up.
When Vidia paused for a moment
Prilla bumped into her and fell
over backwards.

"Watch where you're flying!" Vidia
shouted. She threw Prilla a dirty
look before flying on toward the
laundry room.

Prilla followed. "Well," she called

after Vidia, "at least Twire didn't melt down the crown!"

"That's right," snapped Vidia over her shoulder. "She didn't melt it down. No such luck."

Prilla shook her head as she and Vidia flew to the laundry room. Busy laundry-talent fairies and sparrow men flew this way and that, scrubbing, folding and cleaning away.

Hundreds of chutes carried laundry down to the laundry room from the workshops and bedrooms on the floors above. The dirty laundry fell into baskets. Each chute was labelled to identify where it came from.

Vidia and Prilla found the chute

that led down from Twire's workshop.

A laundry fairy named Lympia was standing under it, sorting through some clothing in a basket. Prilla asked her if she had worked at the same chute the day before. When Lympia said yes, Vidia launched into her questioning.

"Did you find anything *unusual* in Twire's laundry yesterday afternoon?" she asked pointedly.

"What do you mean, unusual?" Lympia replied.

"We're on the trail of the missing crown," Prilla explained. "Are you sure you didn't find a black velvet pouch mixed in with Twire's laundry yesterday?" Prilla asked Lympia.

Lympia started. "Oh!" she exclaimed. "Well, yes, I did find a velvet something-or-other. But what does that have to do with anything?"

Vidia sighed. "The crown was *inside* the pouch, precious," she said, sounding annoyed. "Honestly, if anyone had bothered to look inside the thing, I wouldn't be in this mess!"

Lympia turned again to Prilla. "I put the velvet aside. It couldn't be washed in the laundry. It had to be cleaned specially."

"So where did you put it?"

"Let me try to retrace my steps," Lympia suggested to Prilla.

"Yesterday afternoon, after I sorted Twire's laundry, I picked up a balloon carrier and put the laundry inside," Lympia said. "The light clothes were in one basket. The darks were in another basket. And I laid the velvet pouch in the bottom of the carrier."

They followed Lympia back to the washtubs. "I put Twire's clothes in the water."

Lympia led them to the balloon-carrier storage area. "Then I brought the balloon-carrier back here." She put a hand to her forehead.

"I guess I forgot to take the velvet pouch out of the carrier before I returned it," she said sheepishly.

Lympia had no idea who had
used that balloon carrier next. But
she did have one more piece to add to
the puzzle.

"Yesterday lots of laundry-talent
fairies were washing and folding
tablecloths for the queen's Arrival
Day party," Lympia remembered.
"They loaded all the clean tablecloths
and napkins into balloon carriers.

Then the celebration-setup fairies came to pick them up." Lympia shrugged. "Maybe one of them took the carrier with the pouch in it. Maybe it was hidden under the clean laundry," she suggested.

Prilla thanked Lympia for her help. Vidia was already halfway across the room, headed for the door.

"Hey, Vidia! Wait up!" Prilla called as she chased after her.

Vidia waited outside the laundry room for Prilla. "We've been at this all morning!" Vidia fumed. "And we're no closer to finding the crown!"

Prilla smiled. She patted Vidia on the back. "Sure we are," Prilla said encouragingly. "We're solving the mystery!" Prilla's blue eyes twinkled. "And you've got to admit – it is kind of fun."

Vidia pursed her lips and squinted at Prilla. Then, without a word, she turned and zipped off down the corridor. But before she did, Prilla thought she saw a tiny twinkle in Vidia's eye, too.

They tracked down the celebration-setup fairies in the tearoom. Prilla's stomach growled. She knew that she might not have the chance to eat for the rest of the afternoon. So she helped herself to a strawberry angel-food cupcake from the buffet.

Then, her mouth full, she spotted Vidia already talking to Nora, one of the celebration-setup fairies. Prilla flew over in time to hear Vidia's question.

"Excuse me, honey lamb," said Vidia, turning on the sweetness, "but did you find a black velvet pouch when you were setting up for the party yesterday? It was mixed in with the tablecloths."

Nora was setting the table. Without even looking up, she replied, "You mean the velvet pouch with the crown inside it?"

Vidia and Prilla couldn't believe their ears. Did Nora know where the crown was?

Vidia spoke first. "Yes! Yes!" she cried. "The one with the crown inside it! Nora, where is it?"

Nora looked up. She was taken aback by the excitement in Vidia's voice. "We took it out of the pouch and tossed it in the back room with all the other crowns," she said.

"What other crowns?" Prilla asked.

"The crowns for the party," Nora replied. She put the spoons down on the table in a pile. Then she waved for Vidia and Prilla to follow her.

Nora flew to a small door and opened it. There before them were stacks and stacks of shiny, glittering crowns – and every one of them looked exactly like Queen Ree's!

9

"**They look good** – almost real. Don't they?" Nora said proudly.

Nora picked up a crown from one of the piles and placed it on her head. "They're for the Arrival Day party. We had them made to look just like Queen Ree's real crown. We were going to put one at every seat. Each fairy could wear it during the celebration and take it home as

72

a party favour. But when the queen announced that the real crown was missing" – Nora shot a quick glance at Vidia – "and the party was called off, we left them here." Nora took the crown off her head. She put it back on a pile. "Now we're not sure what to do with them."

Vidia sighed. "Well," she said, "I'll tell you the first thing to be done with them."

Nora looked at Vidia. "What?"

"We'll need to go through them all and look for the real crown," Vidia replied.

Now Nora looked confused. Prilla explained everything.

Nora's eyes widened in shock. "But that means..." Her voice trailed off as she put the pieces together. "The crown in the velvet pouch... the one we tossed in here..."

Prilla and Vidia nodded. Yes, the queen's real crown – an irreplaceable work of art from the earliest days of Pixie Hollow – was here. It was somewhere in this dark, dusty storeroom.

How in the world would they find it, mixed in with hundreds of fake crowns that looked exactly like it?

"Nora," Prilla said at last, "who figured out how to copy the real thing so well?"

"Dupe," Nora replied. "You know, he's one of the art talents. He spent a lot of time getting it just right."

A short while later, a gloomy Dupe stood in the storeroom, in the middle of piles and piles of crowns.

"So," Vidia said to Dupe, "is there a way to tell the real crown from the fakes?"

Dupe nodded. "There is," he replied. "But not by looking at them." He picked up a crown. "You see the delicate metalwork? These rows of moonstones? The large fire opal in the centre?" He pointed out all the crown's beautiful features. "When

I crafted the fake crowns, I used tin scraps and fake jewels for all of these things. But with a lot of fairy dust and some special magic, I glossed over all the imperfections. Now, there is no way to tell that they aren't real."

The fairies looked carefully at the crown Dupe was holding. It was true. None of them would have guessed that it wasn't the real thing.

"I copied the real crown exactly – dent and all." He pointed to a dent on the fake crown he was holding. "There was only one part of the real crown that I wasn't able to copy."

The fairies' faces brightened as Dupe went on.

"When it's placed on someone's head, the real crown magically changes its size to fit the wearer perfectly," he explained. "My magic wasn't strong enough to do that. All of the fake crowns are size five."

"Let me get this straight," Vidia said. "We have to try on all these crowns until we find one that magically fits our heads?"

Dupe nodded. "Oh. And one other thing," he said. "There are

some words you need to say when you put the crown on your head to trigger the real crown's magic."

Vidia eyed him warily. "What kind of words?" she asked.

Dupe cleared his throat. "You have to say:

> 'Pixie Hollow,
> Mother Dove –
> The world we cherish,
> The one we love.'"

Vidia cringed in disgust. "Ugh!" she cried. "That's got to be the sappiest thing I've ever heard!"

Prilla clapped Vidia good-naturedly

on the back. "Well, Vidia," she said,
"it may not roll off the tongue now.
But it will in a few hours – after
you've said it a *few hundred times!*"

10

Vidia picked up a crown.
She placed it on her size three and
a half head. It slipped down and
covered her eyes.

Then, in barely a whisper, Vidia
said the magic words.

> *"Pixie Hollow,*
> *Mother Dove –*
> *The world we cherish,*
> *The one we love."*

Nothing at all. No change. No magic. The crown remained as ill-fitting as ever.

Vidia sighed, took off the crown and tossed it into the fake pile. Then she picked up another crown and tried again.

This went on through the evening and long into the night. At midnight, the unsorted piles still towered higher than the fake pile.

As the first light of the new day peeked through a high window, Vidia paused in her search and yawned. She looked around at the others. Dupe was slumped against a box, sound asleep. A crown was perched on his head. Nora's eyes were also closed. She had stretched out on the floor right in the middle of the unsorted crowns.

Prilla, however, was still searching.

Vidia reached for another crown from an unsorted pile. By now, the task was automatic. Reach for crown, place on head, say words, toss. Reach for crown, place on head, say words, toss.

So when it happened, Vidia almost missed it.

Reach for crown, place on head, say words, t –

But this time, as Vidia reached up to take off the crown, she froze.

Was it her imagination? Or had this crown just... shrunk?

When she first put this one on, it had slipped down and covered her eyes like all the others. But now, as she reached up to touch it, it sat perfectly on the top of her head.

Slowly, Vidia took off the crown. She held it in front of her and stared at it. So this was it. This was Queen Ree's crown. The real thing.

In the courtyard of the Home Tree, Queen Ree tried to start the hearing.

"Everyone, please!" she shouted over the noise. "Please, quiet down!"

The crowd hushed.

"Vidia?" Queen Ree said. "This hearing is your chance to speak to the charge against you. You have been accused of the theft of the royal crown." The queen waved Vidia over, letting her take centre stage. "Let us all listen with open hearts and minds to whatever Vidia says."

Queen Ree took several steps back. Vidia came forwards, her hands still clasped behind her back.

"Well," Vidia said in a loud, clear voice, "I really don't have anything to say." She took one hand from behind her back and held it out toward the queen. In her hand was the crown. "I think this should speak for itself,"

Vidia added with a wry smile.

A cry of surprise rippled through the crowd.

Silence settled over everyone once more. Queen Ree turned to Vidia and took the crown from her hand.

"I don't understand," the queen said. "Don't you want to say anything about where you got this or why you have it?"

Vidia shook her head. "No," she replied. "But, if it is all right with you, my dear queen" – Vidia smiled sweetly and bowed low before Queen Ree – "I would like to call some others up to say a few words."

The queen nodded. Vidia looked

out into the crowd. "I would like to ask Rhia, Aidan, Twire, Lympia, Nora and Dupe to come up here," she announced.

One by one, the four fairies and two sparrow men flew to the centre of the courtyard. Each of them looked somewhat embarrassed as he or she stood next to Vidia.

When all six of them stood facing the crowd, Vidia nodded at Rhia. "Rhia," she said, "be a dear and tell everyone what you did with the crown on the morning of the Arrival Day party."

And so, Rhia began the tale of how the queen's crown went on a long and eventful journey all over the Home Tree. She was followed by Aidan. The tale continued, passing from one storyteller to the next – from Twire to Lympia to Nora to Dupe. Each one explained his or her role in the disappearance of the crown until the whole story was told.

Vidia sneaked a sideways glance at Prilla. Prilla smiled at her – and a strange thing happened. Vidia smiled back at Prilla. It wasn't one of Vidia's fake, sickly sweet smiles, either. It was a real, true sign of Vidia's gratitude for Prilla's help. Prilla knew there would be no thank you. She knew that from this moment on, she and

Vidia would probably never speak of the matter again. She knew that the smile was all she would get.

But it was enough.

Queen Ree stepped forwards to speak to everyone. "Well," she said, "I think that clears the matter up for me. I have no doubt that everyone here feels the same." She glanced around at the crowd. Everyone nodded in agreement.

"There's just one other thing," the queen went on. She stepped over to Vidia's side and laid a hand on her shoulder. "Vidia, I owe you an apology," she said. "We all owe you an apology. To celebrate, I'd like to reschedule the party."

The crowd cheered.

"But this party will not only be an Arrival Day celebration for me," the queen went on. "It will be a party for Vidia, too." She looked questioningly at Vidia. "Will you be our guest of honour?" the queen asked.

Vidia smiled. "Really, Ree, you flatter me," she said. Her voice dripped with sarcasm. "But frankly, I'd rather go on another wild-goose chase, searching for one of your missing baubles, than come to any party of yours." She smiled and took off into the air.

Almost as one, the crowd gasped in

shock at Vidia's rudeness. To say such a thing – when the queen had been trying to make everything better!

But then again, Vidia had never been one to mince words.